# Snippy the Crab's Deep Sea Adventure

## Alison Miles

ISBN: 978-1-915130-00-6

For my family.

To my parents for their
love of poetry, music and art,
and to my husband and children
for all the happiness they bring me.

Snippy the crab looked out from his lair
Over rose-spangled waters and dawn-dappled air.
And though all at shoreline was calmness complete,
He was jitterbug-restless on six JIGGLY feet!

For Snippy a secret held close in his heart;
A life of adventure he'd **LONG** planned to start
And as pearly-pink rays washed his rock pool retreat,
It was time to depart on his far-fathomed feat.

1

So waking his friends to share God-speed goodbyes,
He told them in brief of his bold enterprise.
"But wait," wailed the mussels. "We want to come,
    too!"
"Nice thought," chuckled Snippy, "'cept you're
    stuck fast like glue."
And the barnacles bound in their bony-white cluster
Tried their hardest to move with all the strength
    they could muster.

"It's no good," they called out. "We're ram-
    jammed in this groove.
We don't think we'll ever be able to move.
But is it safe, daring Snippy, to go off alone,
When you've never been anywhere all on your own?"

**"TUSH!"** quibbled Snippy, "I've too long
  dilly-dithered,
A deep-sea explorer can't be lily-livered.
I must be away.
No time to delay!"

And quick as a cod-blink, he scaled up the side,
Tarried a tick for the turn of the tide...
Atop next broiling breaker, he set himself free
And riding the surf was swept out to sea...

Cock-a-hoop Snippy covered the sea's sandy bed,
Chest huffing and puffing, legs **RACING** ahead.
But just at that moment, disquieting quirky,
The ground stirred beneath him; the water turned
    murky.

A funny flat fish he saw racing away,
But it rounded on Snippy and snapped back to say:
"You'd better watch out son; your pincers are prickly.
You walked on my back there and made me quite
    tickly!"

"So sorry," chirped Snippy, "to trouble your rest,
But have you been through a mangle in your
    speckeldy vest?"
"You may find me odd," the fish gloated with glee,
"But there are far stranger creatures out deep –
**WAIT AND SEE**!"

6

Yet despite this alert, he sped on unperturbed;
His thirst for exploring undimmed, undisturbed.
And his mind ran away with image entrancing
Of sparkling sunbeams on warm shorelines
   **DANCING**.

In search of adventure, his legs scuttled faster;
Phantom shipwreck he sought with ghost
   quartermaster!
Till he finally **PUFFED**, "I really must stop.
I can't speed forever like some whirring top!"

Yet as he looked round for a safe place to rest,
His heart **HIPPY-HOPPED** deep down in his chest:
All about him great rocks, lowering, towered,
Each cranny billowed a bladderwrack bower.
Looking up to the surface, no glimmer of light,
In his haste, he'd not noticed the advent of night!

Creeping warily forward, cowed low to the ground,
Senses taut-straining for ominous sound...
When all of a sudden, just there on his left,
A sinister shape streaked out from a cleft...

# SWIPE!
## STRIKE!
### SNAP-TRAP TIGHT!

He was clamped by a claw with vice-like might,
Reeled up by one leg and dangled on high
Face to face with his captor's dinner-plate eye!

Now the lobster's a beast from a time long outdated,
Of infamous hunger that demands to be sated.
With ravenous longing, at Snippy she leered
And in cavernous voice raspingly sneered:
"I'll not waste my time on such tiddlesome fry!
But you'll be gobbled for lunch for sure by and by..."

So Snippy was dropped from her crenellate claw,
And jumbled-a-tumble back down to the floor,
Where all helter-skelter,
He darted for shelter,
And cleaved himself into the cleft of a rock,
Where of his predicament slowly took stock.

All the long night Snippy quaked in his keep,
Appalled by the monsters that dwelt in the deep:
Beasts trailing tentacles, suckered and wobbly;
Gargantuan clams, all gnarly and knobbly;
War-battered crabs of **JUMBOSIMOUS** size;
And shoals of huge fish with cold, **GOGGLY** eyes!

When at length he perceived the darkness grow less,
Though still very frightened (he had to confess),
He resolved to embark on his well-crafted scheme
To decamp from his hideout without being seen.
So clipping some seaweed to cloak him completely,
He slipped underneath it and fastened it neatly.

Then creeping along to a beckoning ledge,
He happened upon this doomed place's edge.
Safety for sure was just a short drop –
His chance to escape this deathly outcrop!
And drifting...down gently...to soft sandy floor,
The moment he touched it with outermost claw,
He ran as if caught in a top steeplechase,
The weed **WHIPPING** wildly his wee carapace.

But the sands that had yesterday filled him with glee
Stretched as far all about as keen crab eyes could see.
Which way should he aim?
It all looked the same...

And he slowed down to ponder
The best route to wander,
When right overhead a DEEP shadow was cast –
Light nigh-on obscured by something quite vast!

18

Down from a height the colossus descended,
And as it came nearer, its huge form extended.
And **FLUMPF!** — The lump landed, spread-eagling
    the bed,
Like a thick fishy futon atop Snippy's head.

"Who's making that noise?" boomed a thunderous
    voice,
And Snippy piped up, having no other choice:
"It's me. Down here. Trapped under your girth.
I'm squashed flinty-flat in this bothersome berth!"
"Oh dear!" blurted Snippy. "Now there's no hope
    whatever.
I'm pinioned true-tight. I'll be stuck here forever!"

Then as graceful as merfolk in torrentine tides,
With one **WHISK** of his wings, the great fish slid
  aside.
"What's this? A wee shore crab out here in the blue?
Do you not know the dangers for young'uns like you?"

Snippy froze in alarm,
But the beast meant no harm.
And he uttered these words
To soothe Snippy's nerves:
"I'm a big fish for sure,
But no teeth in my jaw."
And he opened his mouth most alarmingly wide
Just so that Snippy could peer down inside.

So Snippy explained, without pausing for breath,
How his quest for adventure had brought him
    near death,
And how he was lost with **VAST** seas to roam
With no notion at all how to find his way home.

The manta thought a wee while,
Then beamed a huge smile.
"Your home, I suspect, is Cocklebed Bay.
Would you like a lift home on a broad manta ray?"

So Snippy climbed up on the great creature's span,
And the manta ray swam as only he can.
Mile upon mile they glid through the seas,
Which the giant traversed with effortless ease.

When at length the ray slowed and came to a stop,
Snippy deftly dismounted with a side-shuffle hop.
"It's time for farewells; my dominion ends here.
The bay water's shallow and fishing boats near.

"But you'll be safe now, I'm sure,
This last leg of your tour.
Conch shells mark the way
Right into the bay."

Yet instead of escaping,
Snippy stood **GILLY-GAPING**.
"But I've nothing to show for all that I've seen,
Not one souvenir of the places I've been!"

"But your adventure's a story that needs to be told;
A scare-tale worth sharing with all – young and old.
Recount the brute beasts of the deep's darkest region
And tell of your fears, for the dangers were legion."

"Your friends will be proud," he puffed with
insistence,
"For it takes a brave crab to travel such distance."
And with that he ended his fatherly talk
And streaked out to sea like slick lightning fork.

29

Back at home at the rock pool his friends were asleep,
So he crept into bed without making a peep.
Gazing up at the sky and the gem-studded night,
Tucked up in his lair, all the world seemed just right.

In the morning he planned all his friends to surprise;
He'd awaken them early with day's silver **RISE**.
They'd be happy to see him, for this he knew well,
And he'd need the whole day his story to tell.

Not a sound could be heard the very next day
As sea creatures gathered 'cross the sweep of the bay.
Enchanted they listened, astonishment mounting,
Transfixed by the horrors of Snippy's recounting.

At the close, there burst out a chorus of clapping
With tentacles **FLAILING** and fins **FLIPPY-FLAPPING**.
Snippy glowed in contentment as all there applauded,
By this hearty reception his courage rewarded.

And on chill winter nights and sun-glistered days,
As the manta foretold along strung bracelet bays,
Snippy's tale still lives on and can often be heard,
As Snippy first told it, verbatim, each word!

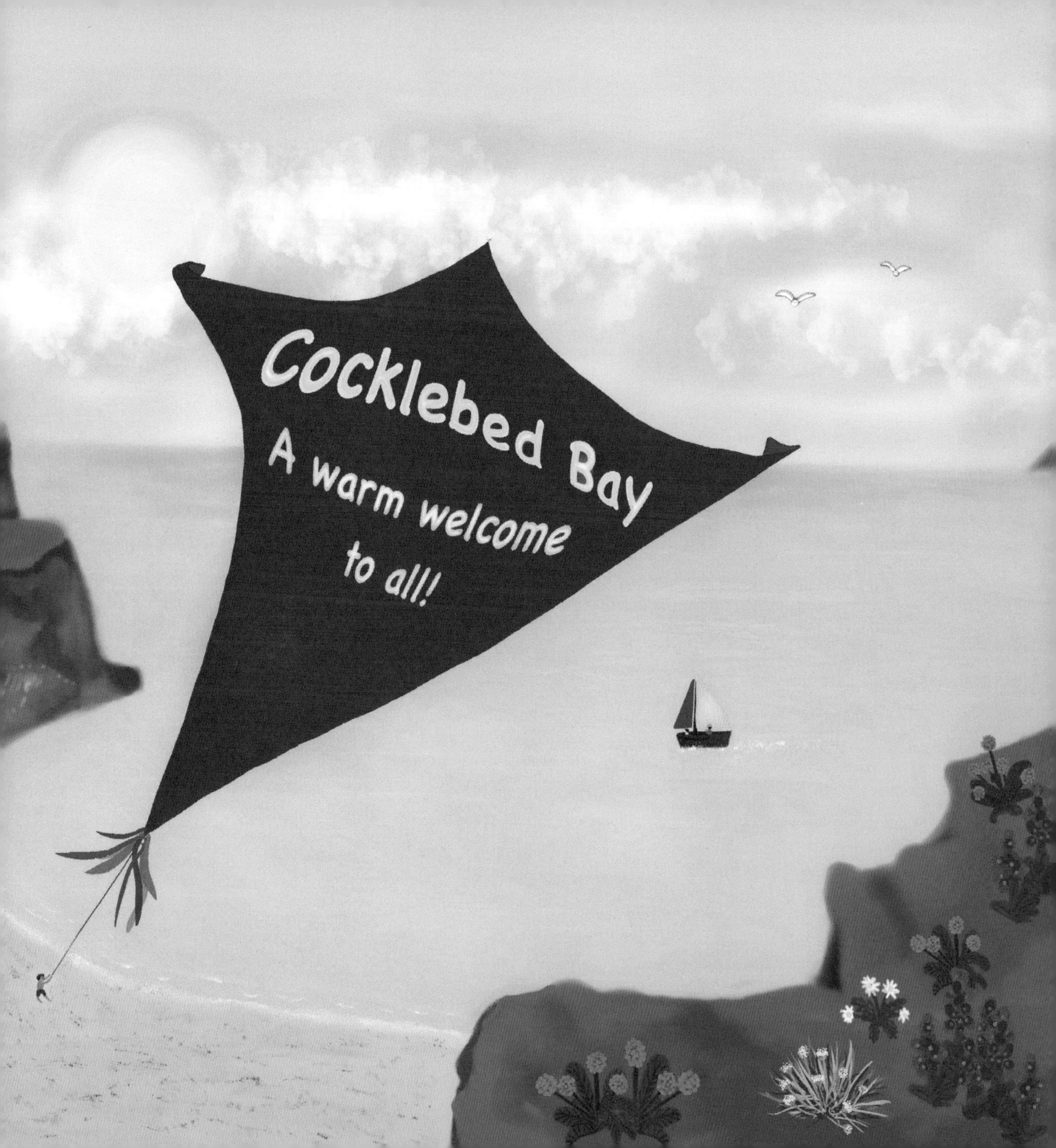
Cocklebed Bay
A warm welcome
to all!

Printed in Great Britain
by Amazon